BUTTS TO THE FUTURE

TIME JUMPER

BOOK 3

HEIDE GOODY

IAIN GRANT

1

---

lice placed a small bunch of flowers on Merrial's grave. They were Merrial's favourite herbs, chosen partly for their fragrance and colour, but chiefly for fixing numerous tiny ailments that Merrial never really suffered from. Whether that meant they worked well, or that Merrial liked to pretend she was suffering, Alice had no idea. Merrial was beyond suffering now, but it helped Alice to think about showing care for her granny through their shared love of herbs. She still hadn't made sense of the events surrounding her granny's death, but with the passing of several months, it was becoming more of a distant mystery than an all-consuming terror.

Merrial's grave was marked with a wooden cross. There were other markers made of stone which would outlast this one, but not all of those had fresh flowers to honour their dead, so Alice was sure Merrial should not feel aggrieved at her station in the churchyard.

Alice held Polly Ann concealed in the folds of her skirt. There was comfort to be found in the familiar bumps of her little wooden body, and sometimes Alice would talk to her dolly, sharing stories about her granny. She heard footsteps behind her and turned to see who was there.

"Flowers must be discarded when they are not fresh," said the curate, Simeon Jenkins. "We must keep the area tidy, as God wishes."

"I just picked them today," said Alice.

Jenkins looked at the flowers. Every part of his expression was disdainful. Alice could not understand how this person claimed to understand the wishes of the Almighty above when he seemed to ooze resentment. "You simply chose poor specimens then."

"I based my choices on the flowers that my granny enjoyed."

"See that they are cleared away before the weekend, and do not use the memory of your granny to justify your slovenly ways. God detests a liar."

Alice prickled with the injustice of his words but said nothing. If she were to point out that there was a world of difference between useful herbs and showy flowers then she would simply land herself in trouble. She lowered her gaze and moved away.

As she walked the muddy path back home, she held onto her dolly and reminded herself of her granny's oft-repeated toast. "Let us have our wits, but take care of how we share them." It had become harder to keep her temper in check without Merrial constantly reminding her that the world could be a dangerous place for a clever young woman with knowledge of healing.

The house was quiet now that Granny Merrial was dead. Alice now only had Polly Ann and Teasel the cow for company. Teasel was not as good a listener as either Polly Ann or Merrial, and had bitten her on the wrist for a spot of inattentive milking the other day. As she came round from the cow byre towards the house, she saw a man approaching on horseback.

He wore a tall hat dark hat, and the pale hose around his lower legs reminded her of the London visitor, Chamberlain, who had stayed with them weeks before and vanished so unexpectedly on the night of Merrial's death. This man's face was more lined than Chamberlain's and it naturally settled into a mask of miserable scorn. He wore a heavy cloak made from the blackest velvet and whisked it over his shoulder to show a glittering dagger at his side.

He addressed her with an intense gaze. "I regret to say that my horse has a small injury. Do you know of someone who might provide me with a healing balm?"

Alice thought that the horse looked well enough. The man was no skilled actor and this was so obviously a trap that she wanted to smile at its crudeness, except that smiling in front of this stranger seemed as if it would be a very dangerous thing to do.

"I might ask at the inn," she suggested. "They are well used to attending to the needs of horses."

"Come come, girl! Surely there is someone hereabouts with knowledge of herbs?"

"Herbs for a tasty pottage, to be sure. I am not sure that I know whether they might be useful for healing." Alice tried hard to look simple and unknowledgeable.

He leaned further forward in his saddle and fixed her with a penetrating gaze. "Well then the horse can wait. I need to speak with Alice Hickenhorn. Where might I find her?"

Alice swallowed hard. This was not good news. "I am Alice."

"Is this your home?" he said.

Without waiting for an answer, he jumped down and handed her the reins.

She tied the compliant horse to the shady tree by the privy and hurried back to find the man was already inside, poking around.

"You must take the taste of your pottage very seriously," he said. "You have harvested a great many herbs." He moved amongst the bunches which hung from the ceiling beams.

"They are most fragrant for strewing," said Alice. She pointed at the floor and trampled a lavender head underfoot, hoping that it would release its smell by way of example.

He continued to conduct his search, picking up a pestle and mortar and turning to her with a raised eyebrow.

"Sir, can you please tell me how I might be of service?" asked Alice.

"Yes." He turned fully and stared at her. "Yes."

Alice had by now realised this man was in the habit of intimidating people. Perhaps he used it to provoke rashness. She resolved not to walk into that trap. She smiled politely.

"Let us sit. I have some questions." He took the chair which had always been her granny's favourite. She sat and laid her hands in her lap.

"Might I know your name and your business?" Alice asked.

"My name is Continent Berwick."

"Continent? That is an ... uncommon name."

"A godly name!" he said.

"An uncommonly godly name," she agreed quickly. "May I fetch you some beer?"

He drank the beer in very tiny sips, as if he was testing for poison. "Your granny passed away some months since?"

"Yes she did. It was a very sad time."

"And on that very same night, a man named Chamberlain was staying here in your byre when he was taken in a most unusual fashion."

Alice was struck cold by his words. They were not phrased as a question, but a statement. "Chamberlain stayed here, but I do not recall his departure," she said.

"No?"

"No. I was concerned for my granny. I imagine he simply slipped away, leaving me to my grief."

Alice could feel sweat prickling her skin, but she forced her hands to be relaxed in her lap, hoping that her face would follow suit.

"That is not the story that Chamberlain relayed to me."

That Chamberlain was alive came as a huge surprise, but Alice tilted her head in gentle query. "I would like to hear that story."

"Oh, you will hear it soon enough. Not here though. Chamberlain turned up in London, confused, filthy and tattered, speaking of demons who dragged him there. The last thing he heard while in your byre was your voice calling his name."

"He what?" Alice's brain tried to process what she was hearing. There was the undeniable weirdness of what had befallen Chamberlain, who had seemingly vanished from his bed with much shouting and no explanation of where he had gone.

"He appeared in London," said Berwick. "Not days later as would a man who had walked or ridden there, but that very night."

"Impossible."

"Indeed. And as a side effect to this grand supernatural event, your granny drops dead. A woman who was reported to be in good health by all who knew her."

"Chamberlain was confused, you say?"

Berwick drained his ale and stood. "He was confused at his situation. I am afraid that any attempt to besmirch his sanity will fall on deaf ears. Both he and I are in the employ of our king. You are aware that the king has strongly held views on witchcraft?"

"I do not have the pleasure of knowing King James' mind on any issues—"

"It is of no matter what you say to me now. I have arranged for you to be taken into custody, and I believe I hear the approach of the men who will take you there."

2

Alice's captors were waiting for her outside the house. All of them were known to her from the town. That they had gathered here so silently for one dark purpose was bone-chilling in the extreme.

Protesting, she was taken by cart into town and thrown into a windowless cellar room of the Swan Inn. She pleaded at the door for the chance to explain herself, but she wasn't attended to for an entire day.

There was a musty pitcher of water on a shelf, but it reeked of staleness, so she avoided it. There was a pail for her to use as a toilet which she also avoided as long as she was able to.

There was nothing on which she might sit or sleep. The earth floor was cold, and the walls were clammy with damp.

During the second day, a servant girl from the inn brought a little food and a pot of ale.

"What can you tell me?" asked Alice, quenching her thirst finally. "What are they saying about me?"

"I am not supposed to talk to you in case you do witchin' on me," said the girl. She had a reedy and high voice, like she had a sore throat and was afraid of hurting it further.

"I won't do no witchin'. Honest. Just tell me."

The girl turned her head so that her headscarf shielded her face, as though Alice might ensorcel her with little more than a glance.

"There's to be a trial," said the girl. "They're preparing for lots of visitors at the inn."

"It's nice that I can improve trade," said Alice bitterly. "But tell me, has anyone defended me and said that I am a God-fearing and honourable person? And not a witch? We don't even have witches in Wirkswell."

"Defend you? There is no one here who will defend you. They will find you guilty. But do not worry. You will be saved."

Alice wasn't in the mood to be soothed by promises of reward in the afterlife. Perhaps the serving girl could see that. "I will bring you fresh water and more food and ale later," she said.

"You are very kind, er..." Wirkswell was Alice's world, but it was home to less than two hundred people. She was surprised she didn't know this girl's name.

"I'm Mandy."

"Thank you, Mandy."

The girl bobbed a curtsey and backed away. "Remember, you are not a depraved and wicked girl, Alice. Remember that."

Alice didn't know how to take that, considering she had never considered herself to be either vile or wicked. "Um, thank you," she said, but the serving girl was already gone.

3

The trial went on for three days.

On the third day, there was an unexpected break in the proceedings after dinner and Alice was returned to her cellar room, where she was surprised to find a table and chair had been placed, with a meal upon it. The guards left her alone, so she sat and ate.

Once again back in the courtroom (which was just the front parlour of the Swan Inn set out as a court with bench seating) Alderman Burnleigh appeared somewhat out of sorts, whispering to various other men, and looking displeased at the answers he received.

"Very well, we will proceed," he said. "Our friend and helper, Master Continent Berwick, is nowhere to be found, but that need not prevent us from pronouncing sentence on the accused. She is found guilty of witchcraft, and in order to serve as an example to all she will be burned at the stake."

Alice's mind reeled. Was that it? She wondered why they had bothered to take a break when the sentencing took about ten seconds. Had they done it for dramatic effect? If so it worked, because as Master Burnleigh declared the session to be over his voice went entirely unheard in the tumultuous row which erupted throughout the room and the street outside. There was theatrical wailing from some of the women, but Alice didn't detect any sympathy for her own plight – it seemed the distress came from the thought of having to watch such a thing.

"You do know I am not a witch, don't you? You also know that you are not compelled to watch me burn? You could just go home." Her voice was also drowned out. Nobody heard her words.

Alice was violently bundled from the Swan Inn. She saw in gut-wrenching shock that the pyre was already built. They had been so certain of the trial's outcome that everything was already in place.

She sought Master Burnleigh's face in the crowd. "Think upon your actions, Master Burnleigh, please!"

The alderman did not even look her way, then there was another face in front of hers: the round pink face of the curate, Simeon Jenkins.

"Thou art a depraved and wicked girl, Alice Hickenhorn!" he spat with fury.

She remembered the serving girl's words. "I'm not," she whispered and then found her voice anew. "I am not! Neither depraved nor wicked."

There was no acknowledgement of her words on the man's face, only a blind and uncomprehending fury.

If this was the true face of Wirkswell, she thought, then it would be better to be dead than stay in it an hour longer.

"YOU ARE a depraved and wicked girl, Alice Hickenhorn!"

Alice sat bolt upright in bed and slammed the laptop shut but it was too late. Astrid Bohart had seen what she had been watching on the screen.

"I ... I..." she began, but didn't know how to defend herself. Instead she repeated "I'm not a depraved and wicked girl."

"I give you room in my house and—" Astrid waved an indignant hand at the closed laptop. "—*this* is how you choose to spend your time?!"

"It was research! I was interested in time travel."

"Time travel? I could hear their ... their orgiastic moanings through the door!"

"And why were you listening at my door? I'm sure I recall a bit of speechifying you did on the topic of respecting each other's privacy!"

"That because I didn't expect a seventeenth century witch to come to my house and—"

"I'm not a witch!"

"—and use my house, my laptop and my wi-fi to watch pornography!"

"Porogoffy?"

"Pornography! Porn!"

"I don't know that word. Can you spell it?"

"P— I'm not spelling the word 'porn' for you! *Porn*! Dirty

pictures of men and women who were probably forced by circumstance to strip off in front of the camera and perform those acts on each other."

"They looked like they were enjoying themselves."

"They're actors!"

Alice frowned. "So Marty McFuck didn't really go back in time to have sex with his mum?"

"Marty Mc—?" Astrid stopped and fixed her mouth in a hard line that held for barely a second before she spluttered with laughter. "Marty McFuck? Okay. What's the name of this cinematic masterpiece."

Cautiously, fearing a trap and more shouting, Alice opened the laptop and sounded out the words at the top of the screen. For the last two week she'd been working hard on her letters. It was helpful that most of the internet was written in big capital letters, like churchyard engravings.

"Butts ... to ... the ... futt ... futturry?"

"*Butts to the Future*, huh?" said Astrid.

"Ah, future. *Butts to the Future*. I don't understand it."

"There might have been a lot of cocaine but very few braincells present when they came up with that one." Astrid gave a mighty sigh. "I'm not impressed, Alice."

Alice bit her lip. "Is it sinful?"

Astrid gave her a disgusted look. "Do I look like an evangelical church minister? Sinful? We don't use that language here."

"Why not?"

Astrid growled. "I haven't got time for this. When you've finished pleasuring yourself to bad porn parodies, you might want to come downstairs and do something worthwhile with your day."

Astrid huffed out and away downstairs. Alice looked at the laptop and put it aside. She was awash with emotions: embarrassment, shame and general annoyance. The twenty-first century was a place of confusing wonders and Astrid Bohart was perhaps one of the most confusing things in it. A woman in her fifties, she was old as Granny Merrial had been at her death, but was physically no old woman at all. She was active and independent and full of the kind of driven energy few possessed. And yet she had the surly manner of the oldest and grumpiest of townsfolk. She balked at the word 'sinful', yet was as judgemental as any person Alice had met.

There was no understanding her.

Alice put the laptop aside and slid out from underneath her duvet. Duvets were superb, definitely one of the wonders of this age. She went through to the bathroom and readied for the day. Toothpaste. That was another wonder. And toilet paper. That was a marvel too. And mirrors you could actually see your face in. And hot water in pipes that came out when you turned a twiddly tap.

The world was full of wonders.

4

Maddie Waites stood outside in the chilling rain and waited for Astrid to open the door. It was actually Alice who answered. She had a bowl of popcorn in her hand.

"I've got news," said Maddie, but Alice completely ignored her.

"Come in. We're missing it," said Alice, hurrying back inside without further explanation.

Maddie stepped inside, slipped off her coat, and shook off the worst of the raindrops. It was only a short walk from the house Maddie shared with her Uncle Kevin to Astrid's little suburban semi-detached, but the weather today had chosen to be especially awful. Which was how Maddie had discovered the second piece of news she had come to share.

She went through to the living room.

Astrid Bohart had, years before, been Maddie's old history teacher, and the living room was exactly how Maddie would have pictured a teacher's living room. The walls were mostly lined with shelves, and those shelves were filled with books and all manner of papery rubbish. In the middle of the room was a sofa and two armchairs, none of which matched one another. It was the living room of a nerdy, over-worked academic. A teacher.

Yet, on this morning the focus of the room was the television in a corner. Astrid's living room was so cluttered, Maddie might have thought there was no space for a TV in it; but there it was, and there was a film on the screen, paused. "*A Christmas Carol*," she noted.

"We're watching it," said Astrid.

"It's nowhere near Christmas."

"That's not the point."

"It might be. Listen, I've come with news—"

"Are you a Christian?" said Alice.

Maddie blinked. "What?"

"Are you a Christian?"

The question threw Maddie more than it should have done. "Um, I guess. I don't know. I was christened. Does that count? I'm not sure if I believe in God."

"Christians believe in God, Maddie," Astrid pointed out, bluntly.

Maddie shook her head. "I'm not saying I don't believe in God. I'm just saying maybe he – or she! – is sort of a universal spirit. Like everywhere but not. Like the cloud."

"A cloud?" said Astrid.

"Not a cloud. *The* cloud. It's like, all around us, but not physically anywhere. Like Spotify. Where is Spotify? It's nowhere, but it's here and it's instantly accessible. Maybe God is like that."

Astrid's coldly unimpressed stare took Maddie straight back to her teenage years in Miss Bohart's classroom.

"God is like Spotify?" she said.

"Um, maybe."

The cold stare lasted a second longer before Astrid turned to Alice. "She's not a Christian. She's just an idiot living an unexamined life."

"Why are you asking me this?" said Maddie.

"We've been discussing morality this morning," said Astrid.

"This time is an amoral one," said Alice.

"From a certain narrow perspective," said Astrid. "This morning I went into Alice's room and I found her—"

"—doing research into time travel!" Alice leapt in. "I've been doing research. We have these woollen bracelets which allow us to jump through time—"

"Right. That's what my news is about—"

"—and I wanted to find out what time travel is. I watched *The Terminator,* which was scary. I watched a thing called *Bill and Ted,* which was not scary."

"And what did I find you watching this morning?" said Astrid sternly.

"I was watching *Butts to the Future,*" said Alice, holding her chin high, clearly unwilling to be shamed by Astrid's question.

It took Maddie a moment to process that. "Right. So, you mean a porn version of...? Right. I mean surely they could have come up with a better title. *Fuck to the Future*? Maybe too on the nose. *Backside to the future*? Meh. Okay. I get it."

"And that has led us on a tour of what is considered moral and immoral in this current time," said Astrid. "Alice getting her head around the notion that we are living in a cheerfully godless society."

"Apart from all the Christians and Muslims and Hindus and Sikhs," Maddie pointed out.

Astrid blew out her lips like this was of little consequence. "They're just a few years behind the curve. But to offer a balm to the degrading filth found on the internet—"

"It's all porn and cats. Although my band has a YouTube channel, too," said Maddie.

"No one cares about that," said Astrid curtly. "So, to provide a little innocent warmth and cheer to Alice's education, we're watching a charming literary classic film adaptation."

"*A Christmas Carol*," said Maddie.

"Exactly."

"The Muppets version."

"It's the best one," said Astrid.

"And you've been explaining to Alice that Bob Cratchit isn't actually a frog married to a pig in the original story?"

"Isn't he?" said Alice. "What animal is he in the book?"

"We've not delved into the details yet," said Astrid. "We're just enjoying it for what it is. And learning a little about Victorian London."

"Oh, yeah," said Maddie. "Definitely historically accurate. You are aware, Alice, that those characters aren't real? Just checking. You know that Miss Piggy's got a man's hand shoved up her backside, controlling her every movement?"

"I know that," said Alice, in the manner of a person who had just learned the fact.

"If you can't buy into the charming world of the Muppets, then I don't see any point in you being here," said Astrid.

Maddie plunged her hand into Alice's popcorn and popped a piece in her mouth. "I came with news. I might have mentioned it."

"Yes?"

"Skid is dead."

"Skid on the motorbike?" said Alice.

"Skid, the bloke with the motorbike. He's dead."

"No, he isn't," said Astrid. "He did die, but we went back in time and waved a pretend speed gun at him and he slowed down and he isn't dead. It's not news if it's a week out of date and wrong, Maddie."

"Yes, I know. He was dead, then he wasn't, and now he's dead again."

"How?"

"He crashed his motorbike."

"When?"

"The day after we stopped him dying the first time."

"The next day? Bloody hell! What happened?"

"Took a corner too quick."

"If he hit a lorry again I'm going to start suspecting the lorry driver has a vendetta against him."

"We should save him again," said Alice.

"We can't save him again," said Astrid.

"Why not?"

"If we save everyone every time they need saving, where would it end? Everyone gets one save. That's it."

"What?" said Maddie. "Is this a voucher system? Why does everyone only get one save?"

"We have our own lives to lead. And our attempts to make some cash on the side from this time travel thing have so far come to naught."

"I know, I know, we're busy. I've got a gig tonight with the band – by the way, you're both invited."

"Not interested," said Astrid.

"I didn't ask if you were interested. You've been invited. You need to get out more and make friends."

"I have enough friends."

"How many?" said Maddie.

"I had two friends," said Alice. "Polly Ann and Teasel."

"Okay, one of them is a badly carved doll and the other was a cow," said Astrid. "They don't count."

"They do."

"Oh, and you have more than two friends, do you, Astrid?" said Maddie. "Human *or* otherwise?"

Astrid pouted. "Irma at the museum. You've met her."

"She banned you from the museum and threatened to call the police."

"That's just friendly banter."

"You have literally described her as your nemesis."

"Friendships are complex things."

"You're both coming out tonight to Backnell to see my band and drink alcohol. And—" she added, waggling her wrist "—because we have the astonishing power of time travel, we can do that and go back and save Skid. Which brings me onto the second thing. I was hurrying over here, and it was raining, and I guess I was thinking about how I wanted to get here quicker, and I suppose I was thinking about only jumping back in time a bit, but..."

Maddie concentrated for a moment, then appeared across the room, staggering slightly. Astrid's and Alice's heads whipped round.

"You jumped!"

"I jumped," said Maddie.

"But in space as well as time!" said Astrid.

"Ta dah!" said Maddie with a little jazz hands.

"Space and time," said Astrid, actually impressed for once. "The universe is our oyster. How did you do it?"

"Huh," said Maddie. "Well, I am not sure how it works, but it's something like a wish or a visualisation. I think hard about the place and the time I want to go to, then *boom*. We're off."

"I don't like this wish-fulfilment concept," said Astrid. "Heck, does that mean telepathy is real? Are our wishes being interpreted? And by whom?"

"Well, I don't know how it works."

"I would say that it's more like a wheel," said Alice.

The other two turned to her with confusion on their faces.

"I don't know my numbers like the two of you, but I can picture a wheel." She used her hands to draw the arc of its rim in the air. "So here's this moment, and there's the moments that we had yesterday." She moved a hand a little way down the imaginary wheelrim. "More yesterdays are this way." She moved the hand further.

"A wheel. Interesting, I can work with that. Nice idea, Alice, thank you. Now what about when we want to go to different places? Can we do that, or do we need to get on a train down to London before we start?"

Alice made a different shape with her hands, feeling her way towards an answer.

"What? What's that you're doing?" Astrid sneered. "Your spellcasting might have impressed people in the seventeenth century, but now it just looks like you're doing *tai chi*."

Alice shrugged. "I was trying to show you how I think it works. It's shaped like a stretchy bone."

"Pardon?"

"A stretchy bone."

"That's not even a thing."

"I'm just trying to describe it."

The other two held out their hands and tried to emulate Alice's movements.

"The wheel is *here*, and it can move distances *here*." Alice's hands twisted in different directions as she tried to explain. "So the distance one won't work unless the time one is moving quite a lot."

"Eh?"

"I'm saying that you can only travel further in distance if you travel further in time."

"You're making no sense at all!" Astrid complained. "You're just doing witchy hand things and I don't get it."

"Nah, I think I see what Alice means," said Maddie.

"Seriously? I know you're just pretending, Maddie, because you're scared of being left behind."

Alice and Maddie both stared at Astrid.

"We won't leave you, Astrid," said Alice. "We promise."

"No," said Astrid. "We don't go off on random jaunts without proper experimentation."

"So, a sort of local experiment is needed," said Maddie.

"Exactly."

Maddie smiled. "Like going back to last week and saving Skid."

"Again," said Alice.

"Yes. Again."

5

A strid checked the news on her phone. Maddie was right. The young man, Skid, (of course the news website gave his real name not his stupid nickname) had come round a corner on the hill going up to Backnell and slid right across the road and through a dry stone wall into the sheep fields beyond.

"The day after we saved him the first time!" Astrid seethed. "All that effort with our pretend speed gun and we bought him a single day of life! The ingratitude of some."

"It was an accident, was it not?" said Alice.

"The man is clearly incapable of riding a bike if he can have two fatal accidents in two days," said Astrid.

"Maybe it's just bad luck."

Astrid humphed. "Well, how are we going to save the idiot boy this time?"

"Same method?" Maddie shrugged.

"Can I be the parish constable this time?" said Alice.

Astrid gave her a critical look. "If you spent less time manually indulging your base urges and more time trying to tame that wild birds nest hair you have, maybe you could play the role of police officer."

"Manually indulging...?" said Maddie. "First up, Astrid, ew. Can you not put images in my mind. And secondly, don't start shaming Alice for being perfectly normal and human. Alice there's nothing wrong with masturbation."

"Language!" said Astrid.

"It's just a word!"

"Before noon? While we're about to watch the end of *The Muppets' Christmas Carol*?"

Astrid pressed play and turned the volume up loud so she wouldn't have to listen to politically correct Maddie Waites using technically accurate words to describe sexual activities. Silence, apart from Kermit singing about the number of sleeps left until Christmas, held sway in the room for five minutes.

"So," said Alice eventually, "if he is a frog and she is a pig, why are their children not half-frog half-pig creatures?"

"Frigs," said Astrid after a moment's thought.

"Or pogs," suggested Alice.

Maddie nodded. "It's a good point."

AFTER THE FILM had finished and Michael Caine's Ebeneezer Scrooge had been saved through spooky visitations and heart-warming songs, they set about their fresh plan to save Skid from himself.

once

"Okay," said Maddie who, like Astrid, was one again dressed in a high-vis waterproof that gave her a passing resemblance to a police officer. "We're going to try to jump back to that Thursday, but we're also going to jump to that spot there. You've seen the picture. We can focus on it."

"Is that it?" said Astrid sceptically. "Just look at a picture and wish?"

"No," said Maddie in a tone that was probably meant to be patient, but sounded nothing short of patronising to Astrid's ears. "We are going to utilise Alice's wheel-slash-stretchy bone visualisation method."

"The ridiculous *tai-chi*," said Astrid.

"If you wish," said Maddie, "but we're going to hold hands so that we don't get separated."

So?

"You if we all end up jumping a hundred feet down into solid rock then at least we'll all be together."

"Exactly," said Alice.

Astrid was unconvinced, but not wishing to be left behind in the skills department when it came to jumping through time, she waved her arms about like the others and focused on the woven friendship bracelet on her wrist. The idea that those simple bundle of threads could somehow power their jaunts through time was ridiculous and—

They were on a wet pavement beneath heavy green trees.

Maddie consulted her phone.

"Thursday morning," she nodded approvingly. She looked up the road. "And we're not far off from where we're meant to be."

"It worked," said Astrid, trying not to sound surprised.

"Where did you spring from?" said a lollipop lady at the

side of the road next to them. The earliest arrivals at the nearby primary school were coming up the road.

"We've been here a while. Surprised you didn't see us," said Maddie, gesturing at her own hi-vis jacket.

"You crossing the road or not?"

Astrid shook her head and pointed up the road, The three of them walked up the hill.

"Why was that woman carrying a standard on a stick?" said Alice.

"Standard?" said Astrid before understanding. "She's a lollipop woman."

"I do not know this word."

"A lollipop is a thing you lick," said Maddie.

"You lick the woman?"

"No. Her sign looks like a lollipop."

"And people lick it?"

"No. None of it has anything to do with licking."

"Or sucking," said Astrid and met Maddie's look. "You also suck lollipops, don't you?"

"There's no licking or sucking," said Maddie. "Her stick. Her sign. It allows her to, er, gives her the power to stop traffic so people can cross the road."

"A great power," said Alice.

"Rubbish pay," said Astrid.

Maddie sighed. "How are we going to get this time travel thing to make money for us?" As Astrid opened her mouth to speak, Maddie held up a finger to stop her. "And no, I don't think we should have to make a second attempt at selling fresh fruit to Georgian gentry. There's got to be a simpler way."

"You never struck me as the materialistic type," said Astrid.

"A woman's got to eat. It's that Maslow thing."

"*In a dimly lit tavern, a hedgehog did appear, A fearless little creature, with a prickly veneer—*" Alice softly sang.

"No, not that Maslow," said Maddie.

"It is a good song."

"Sadly lost to us in the mists of time," said Astrid. "I'm sure if someone had written it down, we'd still be hearing it."

Maddie made a thoughtful noise. "Original lyrics to songs. They sell for a lot."

"What do you mean?" said Alice.

"You know. The words of famous songs. If the songwriter jots them down, especially if it's sort of dashed out in unusual circumstances – like on a napkin or something – they can go for thousands of pounds at auction."

"That's it," said Astrid.

"You think it's a good idea?"

"What? Sorry. No. Wasn't listening. I mean that's it." She pointed. "That's the spot where Skid is going to die."

It was the same bit of wall from the news site article, except it didn't have a big hole in it from where a bike had ploughed through. She was certain. Next to it, just behind the wall, was a large sign: THIS LAND ACQUIRED FOR DEVELOPMENT BY LAMBERT WARIS TECHNICAL. RESEARCH – ENGINEERING – PROGRESS.

"Definitely," said Maddie and readied the hair dryer she'd brought with her as a pretend speed gun.

"And now we wait," said Alice.

"You wait behind the wall," Astrid instructed her.

"Why must I hide?"

"Because you are a bedraggled scarecrow of a woman and will ruin the charade."

"You can be so rude, Mistress Bohart."

"I know. And most of the time people just have to cope. It took me decades to realise that."

6

G rumbling, Alice did as she was told. She hopped over the stone wall and onto the grass on the other side.

The land here fell away in a gentle slope. Uneven grassy fields stretched down to Wirkswell and the river running through it. In that instant she realised this world was not so very different to the one she had left behind.

The sheep in the field before her could have so very easily been the sheep that the farmers grazed on the hills in her own time. Alice liked sheep. They were friendly and pliable, though not half as characterful as a cow. She felt a tight sigh in her chest. Four hundred years of separation from Teasel tugged at her heart.

"Uh-oh," came Maddie's voice on the other side of the wall.

"Is it Skid?" Alice called.

There was a strange whooping that Alice had come to recognise from television shows was the sound of a police vehicle.

"It's the police!" Astrid hissed.

There was the sound of car doors. "Good morning, ladies," said a man's voice. "Can I ask what you're doing here?"

"What's it to you, officer?" said Astrid spikily.

"It was a simple question."

"And I want to know why you're asking."

"Being strangely defensive there, madam," said another man.

"The police shouldn't assume that they can ask people anything and expect an answer."

"Shouldn't they, madam?"

"If we're too polite and let the police do as they wish, then they will start to think it's their right."

"We're just out for a walk," Maddie joined in with a deliberately jolly and friendly tone.

"Just out for walk? With a hair dryer?" said the police officer.

"This? Um, yes. Well, no. We met in order for me to lend the hair dryer to Astrid here."

"No names!" Astrid hissed at Maddie.

"You decided to meet here?" said the policeman. "On a country road?"

"Is there a law against it?" demanded Astrid.

"What we are concerned about is reports of two members of the public pretending to be police officers and waving a hairdryer around at people to scare motorists."

"Scare motorists?" said Astrid. "We're not trying to scare anyone."

"Would you happen to have been playing silly buggers down by the petrol station on the Baslow Road yesterday?"

"Silly buggers, he says!"

There was a sudden engine roar. One of the policemen gave a wordless shout. There was a vile, thunderous crunch of metal on metal, and suddenly a helmeted figure dressed in leather was flying over Alice's head. The man came down hard, headfirst into the field, and rolled across the grass in a messy heap. Sheep bleated and fled further away.

Alice was on her feet and running towards the motorcyclist before her brain even knew what she was doing.

Skid lay on his back, motionless, arms outspread like Christ on the cross. Alice dropped beside him. She couldn't lever his helmet off. She managed to get her fingertips under the edge of his cracked visor and pushed it up. Lifeless eyes in a bloody face gazed straight up at her.

"Oh, no. Oh, no," she whispered.

There were further shouts from the road. There was smoke, and she could see the windows of the police car were smashed. One of the constables was struggling over the wall to try to get to them. Astrid and Maddie just stood there, staring.

Alice stood at the policeman's approached.

"I think he's dead," she said simply, for there was nothing else to say.

As the policeman began talking to his little radio, Alice hurried back to Astrid and Maddie. There were pieces of bike strewn across the road, and a great chunk of it embedded in the police car's smashed bonnet.

"What do we do?" she said.

"Time to bail," said Astrid. She gripped her wrist and vanished.

Maddie looked at Alice, blankly. "I don't know..."

"I'm a first aider!" came a cry. It was the lollipop lady, running up the hill to the scene. She rested her lollipop stick by the wall and, with a surprising bout of athleticism, vaulted the wall and ran to assist the policeman with Skid.

"Retreat, regroup, rethink," said Maddie and she vanished just as quickly.

Alice looked at the man in the field and the people uselessly fussing over his corpse. Shaking her head, she picked up the lollipop lady's stick of power and focussed her mind on making a short jump in distance and time.

She appeared, just as she intended, some small distance down the road.

There was, from up the hill, the whoop of the police siren as the car slowed down next to Astrid and Maddie. Neither the police nor her friends had seen her appear. Alice watched Astrid adopt a stern and confrontation stance.

Down the hill, by the school, the lollipop lady had turned to look at Alice, perhaps confused by another person bearing the stick of power. More importantly, coming up the hill at speed was a black-clad figure astride his bike.

Alice took a deep breath a stepped into the road.

"By the power of the lollipop, I command you to stop!" she yelled. She was not sure if these were the correct words, but she hoped it sounded official enough.

The bike wobbled, its brakes squealed, and the rider managed to swerve round her before continuing up the road at a reduced speed. It braked again as it passed the police car.

While the policemen were distracted, Astrid vanished, followed a moment later by Maddie. And then a figure stood up behind the wall. It was Alice's earlier self. Alice could see the confusion on her face.

"And now you jump back in time to stop Skid crashing," Alice murmured to herself.

But the other Alice did not, and why would she? There was no crash to stop. There was no reason for that Alice to jump back and become this Alice. The two women, past and present, stared at one another. Alice felt a strange tension in her head and a growing sound in her ears, like the buzzing of a swarm of bees. A swarm of countless bees...

"Oi, who are you?" said the approaching lollipop lady.

But Alice could pay her no mind. The headache was expanding in her skull, threatening to pop it like a rotten barrel. She crouched and thought of the soft comfort of the sofa in Astrid's living room...

7

Alice lay on Astrid's sofa with her eyes closed.

Maddie brought her a pack of frozen peas wrapped in a tea-towel to put on her throbbing forehead.

"So where's this other Alice now?" said Astrid.

"I don't know," groaned Alice, eyes still closed. "She could still be wandering around out there. But then— If she doesn't jump back in time then she doesn't get to become me, the me I am now." She patted herself down. "I am still real, aren't I?"

"You're real," said Maddie, putting a reassuring hand on her.

"It's the grandfather paradox," said Astrid.

"The what?" said Maddie.

"Or the problem with going back in time to kill Hitler."

"Hitler's real?" said Alice.

"Of course, he's real."

"Oh, I just thought he was made up for movies. Like Robin Hood or Elvis."

"Point is," said Astrid, "if you go back in time and kill Hitler in order to stop World War Two then you create a world where World War Two didn't happen, and therefore there's no reason to go back in time and kill him. So you are stuck between two states where people will and won't be going back in time to kill Hitler."

"Right, right," said Maddie. "I have to show you something." She went to her bag and pulled out her diary, opening it up to show them. "I keep a meticulous diary. I write down everything, just so I know when I've got time to do everything."

Astrid peered at it. "It says you're meant to be doing music practice right now."

"Okay, I write lists of what I intend to do. It's aspirational. Get off my case. Thing is, I tried to write down what happened the first time we jumped through time." She flicked to another page which was covered in notes and lines, many going round and round in loops.

"That's the diary of a mad person," said Astrid.

"Look. Here." Maddie placed a finger on the page. "You got fired from your teaching job because they found weed in your classroom."

"Your weed," corrected Astrid.

"We'll come to that. So, later on, we only meet each other because you illegally parked your car so you could buy fireworks for your moon landing recreation which— Well, I'm not sure how, but it's to do with your attempts to vindicate your view of history, which was the reason you thought you were fired."

"A gross oversimplification."

"And that's how we met. We only jumped back in time to sixteen-oh-wotsit to find Alice because there exists a picture of Alice being rescued by demons in the museum. And when we did jump back, it turned out that we were the demons. Also, on our way back home, I might have dropped my smokes on your classroom desk."

"You're saying it's all your fault."

"I'm saying that none of this time travel stuff would have happened if not for events which occurred when we were time travelling. It's a loop. It's like, where did the idea that we should pretend to be demons come from? We got it from the pictures and history stories we heard over the years, but they only happened because we behaved that way because of the pictures and stories." Maddie's finger ran in a loop around the page.

"I know," said Astrid. "There's bits that make no sense. It's like last week when we saw versions of ourselves, plus a cow—"

"My Teasel," said Alice.

"—just appear on the lawn. And then there was the bit in seventeen twenty where you, Alice, turned up in a bush – again with a cow, and a man in a stupid hat – to tell me you'd given everyone in the house a sleeping draught."

Alice sat up, lifting the peas from her brow. "I never did that!"

"You haven't done it yet," said Astrid.

"It's called bootstrapping," said Alice. "Yes, I've been

doing research too. It is the same as when Marty McFuck goes back in time and shows Doc Brown the designs for the Fucks Capacitor."

"I think it's called the Flux Capacitor," said Maddie.

"Not in the version she watched," Astrid grumbled.

"And Doc Brown realises that is the missing piece he needs to design a time machine," said Alice. "But if so, where did the idea for the Fucks Capacitor come from?"

Maddie sighed. "Loops, paradoxes. Time travel is full of contradictions."

"We have been too frivolous in its use," said Astrid piously.

"But we have not broken the world yet," said Alice.

"Nonetheless, we must be more careful and use time travel only for vital missions."

"Like going back in time and stealing songs that will turn out to be valuable one day," said Alice.

"Exactly," said Maddie, then realised the time. "Shit. We're late for my gig! Quick! You're driving me Astrid, and we're jumping back a couple of hours so we actually get there on time."

"Hardly a vital mission."

"It bloody is," she huffed. "Flynn will kill me if I'm late for this gig."

"We can use time travel to prevent murder," said Alice. "And it is important to Maddie."

"But what about your headache?" said Astrid.

Alice gave this a long moment's thought. "I think an ale or two would help."

8

M addie's band, *Alice's Demons*, were on the bill at the Blazing Man pub in the nearby town of Backnell. The day-long event was billed as an "Indie Rock Festival" and was accompanied by guest beers from a local micro-brewery with questionable and possibly copyright-infringing names like *Hoppy Mondays, The Kegs Pistols* and *Bitter Sweet Symphony*.

They hopped out of Astrid's small car with a full hour to spare before the band were due to take the stage. Maddie couldn't remember a time when she had ever been so early for a gig.

"Okay, your mission is simple," she told the others. "Socialise, have fun, rock out to our excellent music." She cast her eye over the drinkers, and the musicians who were with the other bands. "But while we're here, we find old musicians who know about any famous people and where they used to hang out. We casually get dates and places where we might find them. Dates *and* places."

"Best if we split up," said Astrid, then she eyed Alice. "You come with me, Alice. We have a lot of educating to do when it comes to music."

Maddie had no idea what Astrid's idea of musical education might be but she supposed she could correct any awful ideas Astrid might put into Alice's head. Holding her black Squier bass close like a dancing partner to get through the pub garden crowd, Maddie approached the outside bar and found Gregory, her band's drummer already there. He had a tasting board of glasses of beer in front of him.

"Getting lagered up before our set?" she said.

Gregory grinned. He had a beautiful face when he grinned, and the fact he didn't seem to know just how beautiful was a wonderful and terrible thing. "It's my scientific duty to try out all of these beauties," he said.

"Pint of *Brew Fighters*," Maddie called to the barmaid.

"Anyway, I'm celebrating," said Gregory.

"Oh?"

"I applied for a job today at that new Lambert Waris place they're building out of town."

"Aren't you supposed to celebrate after you've got the job?"

"It's the first proper job I've applied for in years and actually makes use of my expensive university education. I'll celebrate how I like, thanks."

They clinked glasses, but as Maddie took a sip Gregory put his down. "Hang on. Seen someone. Gotta talk to a man about a dog."

He slipped away into the crowd. Maddie couldn't see the man in question but the 'dog' was almost certainly a quantity of weed. Gregory rarely passed up an opportunity to deal.

Maddie stood with her pint and on her phone googled what some of the most valuable song jottings had been. Paul McCartney's handwritten *Hey Jude* had fetched hundreds of thousands, but Bob Dylan's *Like a Rolling Stone* had blown that out of the water by selling for over a million pounds. What made them valuable?

She'd already jotted some notes on what she thought could be factors.

- *artist still has a solid (and wealthy) fan base*
- *must be handwritten*
- *doodles & personal details are a bonus?*
- *song is a classic*
- *song is written by singer / band member*

"IS GREGORIUS PISSED ALREADY?"

It was Flynn, *Alice's Demons'* lead singer, and the one who took their efforts to attain rock stardom most seriously. A quality that was noble and good, and frequently more than a little annoying.

"He's just trying to relax before the gig," said Maddie dismissively. "We're not going to have a repeat of last time."

The last gig had ended rather abruptly for Gregory, due

to a bout of cannabis-induced diarrhoea. This gig couldn't go much worse unless they vomited on the audience.

"Hey," she said. "Pop quiz. How much do you think these handwritten lyrics sold for?"

"What?" said Flynn.

She explained and tested him on the value of *Hey Jude* and *Like a Rolling Stone*. He half-remembered those and some others coming up for auction, so he scored pretty well.

"I wonder what undiscovered treasures might be out there?" Maddie said. "What do you reckon would be the most collectible?"

Flynn mused on the question. "There were some Amy Winehouse lyrics that her family withdrew from auction a while ago. It would be interesting to see what those made if they came up again. Queen songs written by Freddie would be good. You can't go wrong with Bowie, of course."

"Yeah." Maddie thought about that. Should she add 'artist is dead' to her list? "Those bands with long careers probably all had secretaries and archivists, scooping up all the stuff they wrote."

Flynn nodded. "You want the wild, early stuff that they wrote on the backs of menus."

Maddie leaned back against the bar, wondering how she could pin down a pop star in their early days.

"The headliners are here," said Flynn.

They were a Rolling Stones tribute act called *Keep on Rolling*, whose posters stressed the fact that some of their members were session musicians who had actually worked with the real band at some point.

"A bloody cover band," Flynn tutted.

are

"Most of our catalogue is covers of *Devil Preacher* songs," Maddie pointed out.

"Yeah, we're keeping great music alive. We're not being impressionists." He glanced over at the grizzled, white-haired rockers. "They are hardcore though, they've brought their own booze." Gregory nodded to the tables outside.

"I'm going to say hi," said Maddie.

She ignored the looks of astonishment and walked out beneath a darkening sky. The members of *Keep on Rolling* all had authentically lined faces. Their Jagger looked as if he'd had one of those lip filler treatments, and wore a slick of lip gloss to accentuate his pout.

"I'm looking forward to hearing you play later," said Maddie.

All five of them gave small friendly waves.

"You got a favourite song, doll?" asked a guy who had to be the drummer, as his white hair was combed back in the style of Charlie Watts. He had a London accent.

"*Tumbling Dice*," said Maddie. It seemed like a safe bet.

She got nods all round. "Strong choice."

"So, I guess you must have lived through some classic times? Seen some stuff?" she tried, wanting to take her words back even as she said them. Even to her ears she sounded crass and needy.

"She's calling us old, Kev!" cackled faux-Jagger to faux-Watts.

"Golden age, darling. I wouldn't change a thing about it, either."

Maddie decided to go all-in, so she sat down next to Kev. "I'm working on my, erm, thesis, about what makes certain times and places into creative hotspots. I wonder if you could help me with a few questions?" She hoped they might not notice that she was a little mature for a university student. She also hoped they would not demand too much information on what her thesis was actually about.

"Sure. What do you want to know?"

Maddie was heartened by the group's easy-going friendliness. "Thanks. You grew up in London?"

He nodded. "My uncle worked in a recording studio on Denmark Street. Hanging out there in the Sixties and Seventies was amazing. Denmark Street's one of the places in your thesis, yeah?"

"Oh yeah, Denmark Street, of course!" Maddie would look where it was later. Presumably it was somewhere in London. "What do you remember?"

"Everyone was there. When all the windows were open in the summer you'd hear them all. Jimi, The Small Faces – they were regulars, of course."

"Uh huh, of course."

"I was working with Wayne Fontana and the Mindbenders back then," said the fake Ronnie Woods, tuning the bass on his lap.

"Bullshit, Fran," smiled Kev.

"Was too. I filled in for one session between Ted Lee and Bob Lang."

"Hey, doll," said Kev. "You've heard the story about David Bowie parking up there and living in a van, so he could hang out where it was all happening?"

"Yeah? Did that really happen?" Maddie's ears pricked up.

"It really did. Was a beat up old thing, but nobody cared back then." Kev lit a cigarette and took a long drag as he gazed back into the past, where wild camping in central London was an option.

"I don't suppose you remember any dates?" asked Maddie. "I like to try and picture things very specifically. Visual learner, you know?"

"Dates? Now you're asking. Bowie was definitely around in sixty-four, I reckon. He used to go in La Gioconda. Him and Marc Bolan liked it there, but I couldn't tell you dates. Summertime would be my best guess."

Maddie picked up a stubby ball point that was on the table and used it to write on the back of her hand. *Bowie Denmark Street Summer 64.*

"Such stories." She beamed at Kev. "I could stay and talk all day but I guess you've got dodgy hooch to drink, and I need to find my buddies."

"This?" Kev pulled out a brown paper bag with a bottle. "It's tonic wine. None of us can hack the beer here, so we bring our own. Try a swig, it's good stuff."

Maddie glugged a healthy tot. It wasn't terrible. "Good luck with your set."

Gregory reached out a hand to her as she returned to the bar. "You tried their booze! You wanna be careful of that stuff, it might make you blind."

"Might make me play better," she said.

Flynn gave the pair of them a meaningful look. "Can we just not fuck up the set this time."

"I actually practised today," said Maddie.

"You say that like I should be impressed you did the bare minimum."

"I'm impressed," said Gregory, downing another taster glass. "How did you find the time?"

Maddie shrugged. "You've got to make time for your passions, haven't you?"

9

It wasn't really a classroom setting, but it was close enough for Astrid to be enjoying herself. The following morning she had Alice and Maddie lined up on her sofa while she lectured them about what they might expect to find in Sixties Britain.

Alice was curled up on one end of the sofa, her head leaned against her hands as though it was too heavy for her neck to support. Not so much a paradox-induced headache as a more mundane hangover. They'd had to drag her away near midnight, doing a wild moshing dance to old Rolling Stones numbers, then stop on the way home for her to have a tactical vomit into a hedge.

"Okay, the Sixties," said Astrid. "If we're going to leap to Sixties London to try and snatch some song lyrics, then we need to look the part."

"It's all flower-power dresses and flares, right?" said Maddie.

"Not at all. Most people would be dressing and acting as if they were in a Ken Loach film. Remember, it was only ten years after rationing ended." She pointed to a picture on her laptop of shoppers trudging round a vegetable market wearing drab coats.

"Who's Ken Loach?" Alice mumbled to Maddie.

Astrid saw Maddie shrug and decided to rephrase. "At this time older people dressed in fairly dull clothes because they had been through difficult times in recent years. In London, the younger generation were just beginning the counterculture movement, so they would be subverting all of their parents' expectations with their fashions and attitudes. We will be seeing this with our own eyes."

Astrid didn't see the expected levels of excitement at this. Alice's lack of interest was understandable: she was hungover, she was ignorant of things generally, and all of future time was probably going to appear equally marvellous to her. But Maddie—? Maddie could show a little enthusiasm for their exploration of the past.

Tutting, Astrid turned to more practical things. "We'll need to try and blend in, so we should talk about what to wear."

"You'll need to dress in dull clothes to fit in with the older people," said Alice.

"Correct."

"You should be fine," said Alice.

Astrid couldn't tell whether Alice was being deliberately offensive. Her face was a mask of miserable innocence. "Yes. Thank you."

"Most of my clothes are counterculture anyway," said Maddie. "Should be fine."

Astrid paused. "No band t-shirts, obviously. No rips – because I don't think they did that."

Maddie smiled and nodded. They both turned to Alice.

"What? Will this work?" Alice asked. She flopped the sleeves of the green jumper she wore over the appalling jeggings she'd taken a fancy to.

"No," chorused Maddie and Astrid.

Soon enough, Alice was standing in the short Mickey Mouse print dress that Maddie and Astrid that dressed her in.

"Who is this grinning demon?" she asked.

"It's Mickey Mouse," said Astrid.

"It looks nothing like a mouse. This dress is too small. My privates will be right on show if I bends over!"

Maddie nodded in sympathy, but Astrid rolled her eyes. "Then don't bend over when you're wearing it. It's very simple."

"Can't I put them on underneath?" Alice pointed at her favourite jeggings.

"Maybe with some boots?" Maddie suggested. "You need to be comfortable."

Astrid huffed and grumbled, but she found some boots that worked and they were finally all ready to go. "Before we set off," she said, "there's something we should talk about."

"Yes?" said Maddie.

"It's the mechanics of what we're doing," said Astrid. "We don't really know how it works."

"Yeah, we do," said Maddie. "It's the stretchy bone method. Witchy *tai-chi*."

"Using our hands to express our intent," added Alice.

"It sounds so woolly," said Astrid. "You two seem to be better at controlling it than I am."

"But it works," said Maddie. "Show us that photo you found."

Astrid held up the printed photo of a London street in nineteen sixty-four.

"Okay, nineteen sixty-four," said Maddie.

"Don't say it like you're punching in co-ordinates," Astrid tutted.

"I'm trying to visualise it. It's sixty years in the past ... London... Link arms everyone."

Astrid reached out for Maddie and the world flickered and flashed.

They stumbled apart on an uneven street. Shop fronts lined the pavement. The road was a hodgepodge of dressed stone and dirt.

"See?" said Maddie. "We did it. London."

"This is London?" said Alice.

Astrid breathed in and could smell the low but pervasive tang of coal smoke on the air, plus something a bit more animal.

"London in the nineteen-sixties," said Maddie.

Astrid looked at the smattering of people on the street. The men in their ill-fitting suits, the women in their long dresses.

"I'm not so sure..."

There was a shout. Astrid turned to see a horse-drawn cab bearing down on them at speed. Alice was right in the way. Astrid and Maddie grabbed for her as one. The high-wheeled cab sped by, the trailing edge of it catching Alice's dress and spinning her round.

The women staggered back to the pavement. A string of colourful cockney expletives drifted back from the departing cabbie.

"Not the nineteen-sixties," Maddie panted. "You all right, Alice?"

Alice grumbled, patting herself. "I'm unhurt. I think..."

"Nineteen hundred at the very earliest," said Astrid. "We overshot by sixty years."

The incident, slight though it was, had attracted the attention of some passers-by and a couple was drifting towards them.

"Okay, time to get out of here," said Maddie. "Let's look at that photo again. Right place but wrong time."

Astrid had no sooner taken out the picture to show Maddie than they jumped again, from sunlight to sunlight.

10

They landed on a pavement filthy with litter. Sheets of newspaper blew against Alice's legs as a twist of hot wind stirred them. Shops surrounded them on both sides of the road, although there was no traffic like the town centre of Wirkswell, only people.

"Feels like summer," said Maddie. "Are we in the right place?"

Astrid pointed up at a street sign. "Denmark Street. It's a smaller area than I'd expected. Should make it easier, I guess."

"But is it the right year?" said Maddie. "You were alive around this time, Astrid. Does it look right?"

"I'm not going to be born for several years yet, you cheeky girl," said Astrid.

Alice put a hand to her side where the horse and cab had narrowly clipped her. It was only a dull ache, but there would be a bruise come morning, and the encounter had opened a small rip in her dress pocket. "No dangerous vehicles here then?"

"It will be cars rather than horses," said Astrid.

Alice looked up the road for oncoming vehicles, then nudged Maddie. "Did you say a famous singer was living in a van?" She pointed to a square vehicle a short distance away. A skinny young man was climbing out of it.

"Holy shit!" said Maddie.

"It's David Bowie," said Astrid.

"He's very young."

"If this is sixty-four then he's still a teenager."

Alice couldn't understand why the other two were hanging back. They were bewitched in some way – as though they were gazing upon a holy image. The young man had already started to walk off. They couldn't afford to lose him.

Alice trotted after him. "Hello!"

The young man turned and looked at her. She noticed that his eyes were different colours. That would have attracted a lot of trouble back in her time, could have had him burned as a witch.

"I'm Alice," she said.

He smiled as though that was funny. "Hi Alice."

She didn't know what to say. She pointed at the others, down the pavement a way. "My friend says you're a singer?"

David looked round her at Maddie and Astrid. "Does she? She heard our awful covers of Willie Dixon numbers, huh?"

"Possibly..."

"I don't know what I want to sing, to be honest."

"Do you know *The Prick of The Hedgehog*?" she asked.

His grin widened. "I don't think I do. You think it would suit me?"

"Wait until you hear it." Alice took a deep breath, but she felt a hand on her shoulder. It was Astrid.

"I'm not sure the world is ready for that, Alice." Astrid looked to David. "She's not familiar with your work, Mr Bowie."

"Bowie?"

Astrid faltered. "...Mr Jones. It's David Jones, isn't it? For now at least."

"For now." He smiled as though it all made perfect sense. "Are you her mum?"

"No," said Astrid firmly. "Maybe her exceptionally cool and groovy aunt. But not mum."

"Cool."

Alice drifted sideways. Maddie and Alice were the experts, so she would leave them to deal with the singer. She went to look at his van, wondering what it was like inside. Alice could see through the dirty back pane into the interior. There was a large flowery blanket and piles of clothes inside. It would be fun to live in a van, like a gypsy traveller but without the constant smell of horses.

"Careful Alice," called Bowie. "That panel is jagged and—"

Alice looked down, but it was too late: she'd caught the already ripped pocket of her dress on the rough metal. As she pulled away it ripped loudly.

"Bodkins!" she growled and furiously tugged the gap

closed, as though the simple act of pressing it together would be enough to fix it.

The sound of David Bowie laughing in delight and clapping his hands made her whirl in anger. Was he mocking her misfortune?

"Did you really just say 'bodkins'?"

"Um, she did," said Maddie.

"That has got to be the cutest swear I have heard in a long time. Bodkins!" He saw the rip in her top and his face fell. "Sorry about your dress, though." His head nodded and his eyes closed in thought. "Alice, Alice, you've torn your dress!" he sang.

Alice could see how he might be a good singer, it was a good line. Then a thought crossed her mind. "Oh, I know the next part! When I was young, my ma used to say this: 'Alice, Alice, your face is a mess'!" She laughed and danced around, repeating the two lines.

"It's snappy. I might use it one day," Bowie mused.

"You should write it down," said Astrid. "Quickly, before you forget it."

Maddie nodded. Alice thought the two of them looked a little bit over-excited.

"Come on then, let's grab a cuppa, shall we?" said Bowie, pointing at the coffee-bar nearby. "Never hurts to jot down an idea while it's still there."

Bowie stopped to talk to someone, so the three women found a table. A menu was chalked on the wall.

"A beaker of tea is 4d. It looks like English, but I have no idea what it means," said Maddie.

"Four pence," said Astrid. "We're before decimalisation, so we have pounds, shillings and pence."

"How do they work then?" asked Maddie.

Astrid hesitated.

Alice rolled her eyes. "Five pence is the same as a shilling, and you have twenty shillings in a pound. It's pretty simple."

Maddie studied the menu some more. "So if we wanted a fried egg, a crispy rasher, and fried potato it's two slash six." She pulled a confused face.

"Two 'n' six," said Alice.

"It's like sixteen pence in new money," said Astrid, on firmer ground now.

"Twelve and a half," corrected Alice. She wondered why Astrid was making it difficult. She licked her lips, it did smell good in here.

"I grabbed some coins from Kevin's bureau," said Maddie, reaching into her pocket. "He keeps all the old ones, something in this lot should work."

She tipped a handful of coins onto the table. Astrid leaned in and sorted them into two piles. "Jesus wept! You brought future coins, Maddie! What were you thinking?"

"I didn't have time to go through them!" hissed Maddie.

"Chosen what you're having?" David Bowie joined them, and nodded at the coins. "Pooling our resources, good idea. We can get a plate or two to share."

"Yeah, these are no good," said Astrid, covering up a pile of coins with one hand and sliding it away. "They are, um, foreign."

"Anything interesting?" he asked.

"No. Nope. Very dull."

"Sandra, I need something to write on!" Bowie shouted to the woman behind the counter.

She rolled her eyes, as if this was a well-worn routine. She came over with two pads, one to take their order, and another which she slapped onto the table in front of Bowie. He got to work, making notes.

"Alice wondered if you might write one down for her, too," said Astrid.

"Did—?" Alice felt a sharp kick under the table. She half-smiled, half-winced at Bowie. "Yes, I did. Yes, please!"

"Sure, I can do that." He wrote swiftly.

Another young man in a denim jacket slapped David's shoulder from behind. "Ah, there you are!"

David grabbed the man's arm in affection. "I was just coming."

He finished scribbling the lyrics, tore off a copy, and handed it over to Alice with a smile. "There you go! I hope it makes up for spoiling your outfit, Alice. I've got a party to go to."

The other man, shaggy-haired and barely a couple of years older than David, gave the three women an appraising look. "Party, girls?" he said.

"Girls?" said Astrid, arching an eyebrow.

"Don't worry. We'll have them home by teatime, grandma."

"I like parties," said Alice.

"You've not even recovered from last night," said Astrid. "Dancing to the Rolling Stones until midnight."

"The Rolling Stones were playing?" said the one in denim. "The *I Wanna Be Your Man* Rolling Stones?"

"That's the one," said Maddie.

David patted his friends arm. "Eric here plays with the Mindbenders. Great musician. What's that single you've just recorded?"

"*Um, um, um, um, um, um,*" said Eric.

"Awful name. Great song."

The party was being held in a flat and the attached stairwell of the flat just around the corner. The place was crowded with men and women who didn't have somewhere better to be today.

"Is it the weekend?" said Maddie as they went up.

"You don't know what day it is?" said Bowie.

"Are you high?" asked Eric.

"No," said Maddie, throwing a lilt into her voice to suggest she was open to options.

From somewhere came the not loud enough sounds of blues music. Everyone was smoking, filling the place with a dense fug.

A man held out two brown bottles to Maddie. "Harp or Watney's?"

Maddie took the nearest.

"I've not seen you around," said the man.

"I'm a time travelling rock guitarist from the twenty-first

century," she said. "I've come to plunder your treasures and give you the gift of rock and roll."

"Ha! Good one! A chick guitarist."

"Oh, and one-oh-one lessons in basic sexism. Of course, I can play guitar."

"I'm from the seventeenth century," added Alice.

"I'm not sure they had Mickey Mouse dresses back then, but she does use words like bodkin," added David Bowie. "So it's possible."

"Jesus, Davey, who let you in?" said the man without much animosity.

The trio of women shuffled deeper into the party. "You might want to stop casually telling people that we're time travellers," said Astrid. She took a sip from her own bottle and pulled a face. "I forgot how bad most beer used to taste."

Maddie tried the beer she'd been given. It was warm and tasted like cobwebs in liquid form.

"I like it," said Alice, swigging hers. "Not as good as the stuff back home, mind."

"Home home? Or like *our* home home?" said Maddie. "Forwards or backwards?"

Alice seemed to give it genuine consideration. "There will be no home like the one I had with Granny Merrial, but it's not my home anymore. It's hard to understand sometimes."

"What is?"

"How it all changed. Merrial and I were happy, then there was the peculiar business with the London visitor and suddenly I was witch. A depraved and wicked girl," she said with a pointed look at Astrid.

"I've never said you were a witch," said Astrid.

"You judged me."

"We should live in a world without judgement," said Maddie.

"Amen to that, wild child," said a man with a droopy fringe, appearing out of nowhere and draping an arm across Maddie's shoulder.

She shrugged him off. "Dude. Never heard of personal space?"

"No, but care to take a mandy with me and tell me about it in a darkened room?"

Maddie sniggered. "Wow, does that work often? And what's a mandy?"

The man had a plastic bag with several dozen oaty brown tablets in it.

"Mandys," said Astrid, in surprised recollection. "Mandrax. Ludes. Disco biscuits."

"Grandma is well-informed," said the man.

"The next person to call me grandma gets punched in the face," said Astrid. "They're sedatives. Trippy things. Mandys. You know – *'I'm Mandy, Fly Me'*."

"*I'm Mandy, Fly Me*?" said Eric.

"It's, er, a song."

"A future song?" said Maddie, smiling at Astrid's slip.

"An *old* song," said Astrid firmly. "Popular where I was from when I was a child."

"So, these are a herbal sleeping draught?" said Alice, pointing at the man's dusty drugs.

"Yeah. If you want to get all old-fashioned," he said.

She inspected them with interest. "And you would crush them up to make such a draught."

The floppy-haired creep slid round so he was by Alice's side. "One of these will put you into the sweetest, deepest trance."

"And you've got..." She started to count.

"We can discuss more through there," he said, pointing at a door. "We can get a bit old-fashioned, if you like."

There was an expression on Alice's face, something deep and dark and full of intent, that Maddie couldn't quite work out.

"Sure, let's go talk."

"Alice?" called Astrid as the girl and man slipped away.

"Don't worry, grandma. I'm not going to do anything depraved and wicked."

Astrid seethed. "I don't believe it!"

"I know," said Maddie. "That man has predator-vibes just radiating right off him."

"Do I actually look like I'm old enough to be someone's grandma?"

Maddie blinked. "*That's* your concern? Not that we've just let our friend go off into a closed room with a man and a bag of sedatives?"

"Apparently young Alice does not need our guidance or judgement." Astrid waved a dismissive hand. "We'll give them two minutes, then go check to see if she's okay."

They didn't need to wait two minutes. Less than a minute later, there came a huge bellow and the man burst from the room, wide-eyed and shoeless.

"Magic! Black magic!" he gasped. His eyes latched onto Maddie and Astrid. "She's vanished! She's just vanished!"

Maddie hurried forward, barging past him to look into

the room. There was a child's bed in the corner and a scattering of blankets across the floor, but no sign of Alice.

"What the fuck?"

"What happened to the Mickey Mouse girl?" said Eric, peering round.

Astrid was right behind them. "Flaming heck," she huffed.

"Where she's gone?" said Maddie.

Astrid was shaking her head. "I didn't think. I didn't remember."

"Didn't remember?"

"Mandys," said Astrid and for a time would say no more.

Alice landed in the darkness and her feet squished into soft mud.

There was no natural light about, but even on the darkest night she would recognise the place. She realised that she had lied: this cottage, which she had shared with Granny Merrial, would always be her home.

She hadn't actually intended to come here. There was one place and time she really needed to be with the bag full of mandys, but somehow her yearning heart had brought her here. Right now her earlier self and Granny Merrial were sleeping in that house, while over in the byre was a certain Master Chamberlain, a visitor from London. This was the night Granny Merrial would die.

There were voices coming from the byre. Chamberlain was talking to someone.

Alice sneaked around. The door was the only entrance to the cow byre, but on the far side there was a broken plank creating a narrow window into the space. She stepped over the uneven ground until she could put her eyes to the hole.

There was the light of a single candle within, and by that light she could see two figures.

The young visitor from London stood warily, his hand hovering near the knife on his belt. "The fact that you have stolen out here in the witching hour to speak with me says much about you, sir."

"I would know why you have come here," said the other man. It took Alice but a moment to recognise his voice. It was the alderman, Master Burnleigh!

"I have been tasked with asking you several questions, Roger Burnleigh."

The alderman shifted, and now Alice could see his bearded face in the candlelight. "Then ask away and have done with it."

"You have lived here all your life," said Chamberlain.

"That is not a question."

"I have seen a letter, marked with the seal of Good Queen Bess herself, awarding lands to a Roger Burnleigh in fifteen seventy-two."

"My grandfather," said Burnleigh.

"And there is a mention of a Roger of Burnleigh carrying Henry Tudor's standard at the Battle of Bosworth Field."

"A great grandfather, I believe. I wouldn't know. It was over a hundred years ago."

"And yet there is no mention of this grandfather or great grandfather in the parish records of Wirkswell, sir."

"You've looked, have you?"

"I have it on good authority."

"Then you haven't looked. Perhaps I could arrange for us to look together."

"I must know who you are, sir!" Chamberlain shouted. "Robert Cecil himself has directed me to find out."

"His majesty's spymaster? I am no spy!"

Teasel mooed in bovine alarm at the raised voices.

"Spy? Witch? Demon? Is there some title or designation passed from one man to another?"

Burnleigh's laugh was light, conciliatory, but Alice could hear the sharpness in it. "There is no mystery here, Master Chamberlain. All can be settled if you come and look at certain letters I have at my home."

Chamberlain now openly placed his hand on his knife. "I am not the first one sent to speak to you."

"The first I know of," said Burnleigh. He took a step towards Chamberlain and the man backed off.

"Do not harm me!" Chamberlain warned.

"Are you well, Master Chamberlain?" the earlier Alice called from the far side of the byre.

Later Alice, crouching by the broken plank, could picture her younger self with ease, standing outside the byre, armed with naught but a pitchfork.

Chamberlain turned to the door. "Alice?"

With the man distracted, Burnleigh leapt at him and wrapped his arms around him. The two struggled, and from nowhere a wind whipped up around them, as though borne from their scuffle. The door rattled in the sudden gale, and in a blast of wind that threw Alice from her peephole, the two men vanished.

She could hear Alice and Teasel within the byre now, and then the sound of Merrial's voice.

"What has occurred?"

The words stabbed right through Alice. To hear her granny speak again, so many, many months after her death – a death that was going to seize her right now, this night... Alice blinked tears and realised she simply could not be here.

She jumped.

13

S ame spot, different day. Alice's mind had leapt forward, and she knew this was a time into the future, following the trackways of her own life.

She picked herself up and walked round to the front of the byre. It was empty. Teasel was down in the fenced off paddock. The cow saw her, gave a deep greeting, and ran over to meet her. Her teats were bulging painfully with milk.

"Of course, my love," said Alice and went to fetch the milking stool.

Months had passed since Merrial's death and, if Alice was absent, then it probably meant she was either arrested, or had already vanished to the future. Before she had even finished milking the cow, Alice had resolved to go into town and find out exactly what was going on. She had nothing to fear, she told herself, for she had the power to jump away in time in an instant.

She was currently wearing her short dress, which locals

of this time would have deemed scandalous, so she went inside, found a dress that was not too dirty and a shawl to put about her head and shoulders. There was the stink of sweat and ordure on the clothes and Alice thought it funny she had not noticed that smell in her earlier years. The future had already changed her.

She walked into town. The air was cold but the sun was bright, and the sound of the market traders in the town drifted out to greet her. This was not as loud as the constant humming background noise of future Wirkswell, but it was somehow more intrusive, more personal. It was odd how the future was more populous yet seemed to have fewer people in it.

She stopped near the river and smeared mud on her face to conceal some of her features, then wrapped her shawl more tightly about her to shadow her face. The town was alive with trade, the area around the Swan Inn especially busy. It would not do to have folks recognise her as the Alice Hickenhorn they thought they had arrested. Furniture was being moved around in the front room of the inn. The trial had not yet begun. That meant her earlier self was in the inn's cellar, alone, confused and afraid.

The bag of soporific pills was secure in Alice's inner pocket, alongside the lyrics written by Mr Bowie. Would it be so hard to wait for nightfall, somehow give a sleeping draught of mandys to the people in the inn and rescue herself? But no – that was not what happened. If she rescued herself now there would be no need for Astrid and Maddie to rescue her, no trip to the wondrous future. She had only just recovered from the headache the simple business with the motorbike and lollipop stick had caused her. Her purpose here was different.

She went inside and approached the landlord.

"Sir," she said, adopting a strangled, higher-pitched tone than her true voice. "The witchfinder has told me to take food and sustenance to the prisoner."

"Oh, has he?" said Master Harper.

"Master Berwick said she must be fit to stand trial in the morning."

"You have coin?"

"He said a pious man would serve God's servants without question, so that he might not wonder why you had reason to sneak up to the woods on the Burnleigh estate of a night."

The landlord look shocked and hurried to get one of the serving girls to put together a small tray of food. Alice took it and descended into the cellar.

"For the prisoner," she said to the guard at the bolted door. "And who's to say it isn't poisoned?" she added as his fingers twitched over the piece of cheese on the tray.

He let her in. Alice Hickenhorn was squatting in the corner of the room, watching her with suspicious eyes. Alice held the tray forward, explanation enough, and placed it on a beer keg.

Her younger self set upon the food and drink with speed. She drank half the pot of ale in an instant.

Younger Alice wiped her wet mouth with the back of her hand. "What can you tell me? What are they saying about me?"

"I am not supposed to talk to you in case you do witchin' on me," Alice replied.

"I won't do no witchin'. Honest. Just tell me."

Alice held herself at an angle, making sure her face was not revealed. "There's to be a trial. They're preparing for lots of visitors at the inn."

"It's nice that I can improve trade," said the prisoner miserably. "But tell me, has anyone defended me and said that I am a God-fearing and honourable person? And not a witch? We don't even have witches in Wirkswell."

"Defend you? There is no one here who will defend you. They will find you guilty. But do not worry. You will be saved."

The prisoner seemed unimpressed with that. Alice picked up the tray. "I will bring you fresh water and more food and ale later."

"You are very kind, er..."

Alice's mind went to the drugs in her pocket. "I'm Mandy," she said.

"Thank you, Mandy."

Alice curtseyed, then felt compelled to speak. "Remember, you are not a depraved and wicked girl, Alice. Remember that."

14

Alice visited twice more before the trial began, eventually making sure her younger self had rushes to sleep on and a blanket to cover her.

On the first day of the trial, Alice was able to sneak into the back of the room in the inn and find a place from which to observe proceedings. The inn was packed tighter than it had ever been. The prisoner was brought out and a bedraggled Alice blinked at the brightness of the light as though it made her eyes ache.

Outside there was a large, restless crowd composed of people who had not managed to get into the inn. The calls of street vendors drifted indoors:

"What are the signs that you're living with a witch? Buy this pamphlet with details of how you can check."

"Firewood bundles for sale. Take part in the cleansing ritual and earn yourself a place in heaven!"

The prisoner was placed on a seat at the front of the grand wooden benches where the rich folk sat.

This was the second time Alice had been here, but she had not taken in much of it the first time. She had been tired, frightened and bewildered, but now – as a detached visitor from the future – she could observe it all the more clearly. At a raised table at the front of the room sat Master Chamberlain, returned again from London, and Master Continent Berwick, the witchfinder. The two outsiders were dressed in rich clothes, with immaculate white collars. Master Burnleigh wore a finely stitched cloak over his regular patterned tunic. The three men were raised above all others. Alice felt the sharp contrast between their pristine confidence and the parochial grubbiness of Wirkswell folk. She saw her earlier self trying to sit up tall and proud. Oh, she had recognised the power games the witchfinder had been playing first time round.

Berwick tapped a little wooden hammer he had brought with him to draw the room's attention. "We intend to satisfactorily answer the question of whether this young woman is a witch." He was talking to the room generally, but Alice noticed he seemed to be mainly addressing Chamberlain and Alderman Burnleigh. "We will hear evidence gathered by key witnesses, and experts who have been kind enough to travel here for our benefit."

The first witness was Chamberlain, who introduced himself as someone in the employ of King James, although he never revealed what it was he was doing in Wirkswell.

"I had concluded my business for the day and was asleep

in the byre adjoining the cottage which the accused shared at the time with her granny."

"Did you detect any animosity between those two people?" asked Berwick.

"Aye. The girl seemed uppity. Had designs on grander things than a shared cottage from what I saw."

A rumble passed through the room, and the message was relayed outside to those who could not hear.

"That is not true, sire! When do I get to say my piece?" the prisoner Alice shouted.

"Silence!" roared Berwick. "You will be silent in my courtroom unless asked to speak, Satan's servant! And it is most unseemly to address your betters in that manner." Berwick turned to Chamberlain. "Pray continue."

"I slept in the byre until I woke in the darkness, hearing and feeling a great wind take hold of me. It was as if I was swept away by this most ferocious wind, with hands a-grabbing at my arms. The very last thing that I consciously heard was the accused shouting my name. After that I remember nothing but blackness until I awoke."

"And where were you when you awoke?"

"Near to the river in London, in sight of the great tower. I was draped across a low wall, like a drunken vagrant. It was most distressing. My clothes were a-tatter. I presented myself at the tower, where I am known, of course, and they helped to revive me a little. It was then that I became aware of the most astonishing fact." Here he paused, to make sure the entire room was listening. "I had awoken on the very morning when I should have been here in Wirkswell. I had travelled all that way as if in a dream, and it had taken no time. No time at all."

The room erupted with noise as everyone had something to say about Chamberlain's incredible story, and the details were shouted out to those in the street.

Alice wanted to jump up and shout "Master Burnleigh did it! He did it! He took him away!" but she held herself still. She was here to witness, to learn, not to intervene.

Berwick was speaking now. "Upon hearing this account, our king took a personal interest. As you know he has a fervent wish to rout out all servants of the Devil, so he sent me here as his personal representative in this matter. I have considerable experience and expertise when it comes to recognising witches."

"You spoke to the witch woman?" said Master Burnleigh.

"Her manner was devilish slippery when questioned," said Berwick. "I found herbs and the tools for their preparation in the cottage. It is my belief that she is versed in herbal lore and that she lies about the circumstances of her granny's demise. Given that it came at the same moment as Chamberlain's abduction, it is reasonable to assume that she sacrificed the life of her granny to summon the demons which took him away."

The observers in the court became animated at the evidence piling up against Alice. A stern tapping of the hammer was needed to quieten the room.

"She clearly bears a mark of the devil on her arm," continued Berwick. "I have seen such marks before on those convicted of witchcraft. Raise the arm of the accused that we might view the mark!"

Alice knew a rat had bitten her earlier self while she slept in the disgusting cell, but she hadn't been able to treat it. The mark on her arm was slightly swollen. A decent honey dressing might have done something to alleviate the redness, but there was no hiding it.

The prisoner raised her own arm, trying to shake off the painful grip of the guards at her sides, but it was impossible. "It is a rat bite sire, since I am kept captive in a hovel!"

"Silence! I will not have this court corrupted by your sly words, now we have proof that you are indeed the devil's agent. But there is more to be learned. We shall gather further testimony and make sure, to our own satisfaction, that there are no more witches in this fair town."

The witchfinder rose and the other men rose with him.

Even now, second time round, Alice could not understand how this matter had come to be blamed on her. Chamberlain was right there, an arm's length from the man who had assaulted him and whisked him away. Had his mind been addled? Had he been bribed to speak falsehoods?

Alice returned to her old cottage to milk Teasel and to think things through.

It was no hardship to hop forward in time, from evening to morning to evening, to tend to the cow and to drop in on her earlier self in disguise to offer food and what succour she might. Alice could not decide if she was a master of disguise to not be identified by her earlier self, or if her earlier self was an unobservant fool.

On the evening of the third day, when the court had retired for dinner, Alice hopped back to the cottage to tend to Teasel once more, but as she sat down to milk the cow in the byre, she was surprised to hear chatting voices approach the property.

"The crown will seize her property," said Master Burnleigh.

"The crown?"

"Oh, I assume so," said Burnleigh airily. "We will place the deeds in your hands, Master Berwick, relying on your good and honest nature to see the property disbursed in a fitting manner."

Berwick chuckled. "It is an ugly hovel for sure, but the land will be worth enough."

"I thought you might say that." Beyond the closed door to the byre, Alice could hear Burnleigh come to a halt in the middle of the yard. "I was impressed with Master Chamberlain's testimony."

"Ah, a difficult man to influence."

"Really?"

"A truly honest man who struggled to see God's larger plan. He took some persuading."

"I see."

"But he eventually understood that the nation's struggle against witchcraft was more important than any trifling issue of mistaken identity. Who cares if your family tree is a little ... indistinct."

"As you say. Please, explore. Be certain that this is reward enough for all your good work."

The voices moved on. Alice looked at Teasel.

"They lied. They knew they were lying and they lied all the same. That Master Burnleigh sent me to the pyre knowing I was—"

There was the crick of the stiff byre door opening. Alice had no time to hide. The witchfinder Berwick poked his head in disinterestedly and was about to withdraw when he saw Alice.

"What are you doing here, girl?" he said. The brow beneath his dark hat creased in confusion. "You. You look just like the Alice girl."

"A funny thing that," said Alice.

The frown deepened. "You are locked in the cellar of the inn."

"I am."

He strode forward and grabbed her wrist. She recoiled at his touch.

"Master Burnleigh! Alderman! I have the girl here!" he shouted.

"You would have me burn for something you knew Master Burnleigh did," she said softly, the anger burning low but hot within her.

"You used witchcraft to free yourself," he said as though it was a blinding revelation. "Is this creature your familiar? Is this the Wicked One in disguise?"

Teasel was many things. She was proud and gentle, and an excellent listener. But she was definitely not Satan in cow form.

"We shall have it tossed upon your fire with you," said Berwick.

"You'll do no such thing!" said Alice.

The door was opened again and Master Roger Burnleigh, alderman of the town, stared in at them. Alice saw the red and white knitted tunic he always wore, made from the same threads as the bracelet around her wrist. With her own eyes she had seen the man leap away through time with Master Chamberlain. He had the same power as her and, as such, he was the greater threat to her.

She placed a hand on Teasel's side and, with Berwick still gripping her arm, leapt away. She knew exactly where to go.

15

Maddie and Astrid lounged on a threadbare sofa in the corner of the flat off Denmark Street. They spoke openly of what had just happened to Alice. No one around them seemed to care about their talk of time travel. Maddie supposed half of the people thought they were high while the other half were high themselves.

"So, you think Alice has gone to the seventeen hundreds?" said Maddie.

"The business with the pineapples, yes. You and Alice were drugged by the house steward. We only got you out of there because of Alice."

"Who was drugged?"

"No, not that Alice. *Our* Alice. The one who just left. She's got a bag of Mandrax tablets."

"Right."

The more than a little creepy man who had escorted Alice into a darkened room with the offer a few trippy sedatives had long since left the party, shouting that he was going to report the theft to a policeman. Maddie hoped he stopped and thought long and hard before telling a copper he'd had his illegal drugs stolen.

"And that's why you think she's now gone there?" she said.

"Exactly," said Astrid. "Look, the thing with Skid's death and the lollipop lady, and the time paradox that should have ripped a hole in the universe but only gave her a headache – I think she's taken it to heart. The moment she heard the mention of mandys and knowing what I'd heard her say in the bush—"

"*She* knew what *she'd* said? What bush?"

Astrid tutted. "*Our* Alice. I told her what had occurred when this Alice – the one who's gone off now – appeared in a bush outside Burnleigh Manor in seventeen thirty. And the words she told me then convince me that *this* is the moment when she goes there. That's where she is now. Well, not now. Then. The now that is then. I think we need a new vocabulary."

"So," said a guy on the next seat over, emerging from a stupor, "you're a time traveller *and* a lady guitarist?"

"Just a guitarist," said Maddie.

"Huh. So, what's music like in the future?"

Maddie shrugged. She clicked her fingers at a man noodling on his acoustic guitar and gestured for him to pass it over. "Name a decade," she said.

"What?"

"A future decade. Name one."

"The nineteen eighties," he said. "No. The nineties."

"Okay." Maddie flexed her arms and strummed the powerful opening chords of *Smells Like Teen Spirit*. She stopped and looked at Astrid. "But what exactly did Alice tell you? What makes you convinced that's where she's gone?"

"Well, she stepped out of this topiary rabbit bush and said—"

"THIS IS TEASEL," Alice said to Astrid by way of introducing her cow in the darkness of the garden.

Master Berwick was in a perpetual state of shock. "By God! Another witch?"

"And this is Master Continent Berwick, the witchfinder who tried to have me burned," said Alice.

"What?" said Astrid, barely visible in the dark garden despite being in a voluminous Georgian ball gown.

"The evidence of devilry mounts before my eyes!" Berwick cried out.

"Shut up!" Astrid snapped at Berwick and looked at Alice. "To repeat: What? How can you be here?"

"It's a long story," said Alice.

Down by the house, people were coming out into the grounds, no doubt beginning their search for Astrid.

"Are these the gardens of hell?" Berwick asked.

"The short version of the story, please," said Astrid.

"I went back in time," said Alice.

"For a cow and witchfinder? Sorry – did you say his name was Continent?"

"An honest and God-fearing name!" the man declared.

"I went back, used some mandys to make a sleeping draught and gave the potion to the evildoers in the kitchen some time ago."

"Mandys?"

Alice frowned. It was Astrid herself who had told her the word. "Mandrax. That's right, isn't it? *I'm Mandy, Fly Me*."

"Who ... who ... how do you know *I'm Mandy, Fly Me*?"

"You mentioned it."

"When?"

"Nineteen sixty-something. Time travel is very complicated."

Astrid gestured down the hill. "And how did you know which ones were the evildoers?"

"I assumed they all were. They should be sleeping very, very soon."

Indeed, down by the house, people were already staggering about and falling to their knees. Alice had ground up the entire bag of mandys and distributed them among various pitchers an hour before. A peasant girl could pass unnoticed through any fine house if she knew how to walk.

"Now," she said to Astrid. "I can't help you with the next part because I don't want to meet my other self. You need to go in there, attempt to steal the silverware that is rightfully ours and get Maddie and the other Alice back out here. The carriage will be waiting. You have about fifteen minutes."

Astrid was resistant. Alice knew she didn't like someone else knowing more than her. It was sweet in its own way.

"Are you certain you drugged everyone? How do you even do a thing like that?" said Astrid.

Alice winked. "I did and I will show you later. No more

dallying." A clap of her hands to urge Astrid into action, and Alice jumped again.

It was a short hop into the future and to the house. Men and women lay in sleeping poses on the lawn. A couple were still resisting, crawling around on all fours, trying to stay awake.

Alice stepped over them and went indoors, where bodies were also spread around. She had no notion of the lasting effects of the mandys sleeping draught. Perhaps they would wake in the morning and assume they had all had too much to drink. Perhaps.

She stepped over the splayed limbs of fine men and women in the hall, making her way towards the current Master Burnleigh. He was as insensible as the rest of them, curled up like a sleeping baby on the floor. She rolled him onto his back and regarded his face. There was no doubting it: this was the same Master Burnleigh who had lived in her own time.

"What games do you play?" she pondered.

Roughly she hoisted him up and leaned him against a table. She pulled off his fine coat and inspected the woollen tunic he wore underneath. Its threads did indeed match those of the friendship bracelet she wore, but surely it could not be the same tunic. Even the finest, long-lasting wool would not survive four hundred years in good condition.

She knew this mystery was not yet solved, but meanwhile she would take this man's power from him. Dealing with his sleeping body was cumbersome and difficult, but it was less than a minute's work to have the woollen tunic up over his neck and pulled free.

She bunched it under her arm and contemplated what punishment she should give to a man who, a hundred years earlier, had condemned her to burn. She could leap to the dark, distant past, when England was naught but Roman soldiers and godless savages, and leave him there. She could leap to the far sea and drop him off a cliff.

"What are you doing?" came a shout. There was a servant boy in the door to the hall.

"You should be asleep," said Alice, surprised.

"Should I?" he said, equally surprised.

She guessed not everyone would have drunk from the poisoned pitchers after all. She pointed at the comatose Roger Burnleigh. "You tell him he is a lucky man. He would have seen me burn at the stake, but I let him live this night."

The boy didn't understand, yet she could tell he would pass on the message. "Who are you?" he said.

"I'm Marty McFuck," she said. "Now, stand back now, for I am about to perform witchcraft."

She jumped again, once into the gardens to find Teasel, and a further jump to a distant future.

16

Maddie was working her way through a repertoire of future rock staples and was about to play the opening riff of *Seventh Nation Army* when Astrid said, "Aren't you worried about depriving future musicians of the chance to write these songs for the first time? If you play it and this lot hear and remember it, they might steal it for themselves several decades too early."

Maddie was less bothered, although that might be due to the three beers coursing through her body. "All creative endeavour is an act of plagiarism. Did Radiohead write *Creep,* or did they rip it off an old Hollies song? Is the Beatle's *Come Together* an original or a blatant steal from Chuck Berry? The true genius of music is in the execution."

The young David Bowie, so slender and intent, leaned forward, waiting for Maddie to play again when, above the music and general hubbub of the party, there was a sudden and definite thump from the nearby bedroom, followed by a loud moo.

"Did you guys hear a moo?" said David.

"I heard a moo," said Maddie. "Did you hear a moo?"

Astrid fought her way out of the bean bag she was sprawled in and moved hesitantly towards the door. "I definitely heard something."

"Has Mickey Mouse girl turned into a cow?" asked a partygoer.

The door was flung open and Alice stepped through with a red and white jumper under one arm. Her face was smeared with mud and she had rough woven clothes wrapped over her dress. Behind her, in the bedroom, there was definitely a cow. It was a brown cow and appeared to be as confused as to why she was in a first floor bedroom in London as the rest of them.

"This is far out," said David. "I've not even taken anything."

Alice looked to Maddie and Astrid. "Sorry. I had to pop out."

"Slip some mandys into some drinks and rescue your cow," said Astrid. "When you said, *I'm Mandy, Fly Me*, I knew this was the time you'd met me in the grounds of Burnleigh Manor."

"I'm Mandy, Fly Me," said the young musician, Eric. "Such an odd phrase."

"It will make sense eventually," said Astrid. "Time for us to go, I think."

"What happened, Alice?" said David. "Your face really is a mess."

"Keep working on those lyrics," said Maddie as the three of them moved towards the bedroom door. "We'll look you up when it's a big hit."

"If you're leaving," said David, "the stairs are that way."

"We're very unconventional," said Maddie and shut the bedroom door behind them.

It was a very small space with a large cow in it.

"Everyone, this is Teasel," said Alice, proudly.

"You thought you'd bring your pet cow with you?" said Maddie.

"We've seen her before," said Astrid. "Everyone hold hands. Or hoofs. Or whatever."

Maddie focussed on the future and Wirkswell. "Ready?" she said and, without waiting for a reply, they jumped—

—From a darkened room to a garden in bright daylight. It was Astrid's front garden. Maddie was about to congratulate herself on hitting the target first time when she saw the trio of women coming up the driveway. It was themselves. Astrid was carrying a bulging shopping bag.

The Alice on the driveway pointed at them. "That's my cow!"

"What's happening?" Alice hissed at Maddie.

"Clearly too early!" Maddie hissed back. "This is last week before Astrid did her Lady Gaga thing."

The Astrid on the driveway solemnly raised her hand in greeting. "Well met, fellow travellers."

The Astrid on the lawn returned the gesture. "Well, met."

Maddie grabbed Astrid and jumped again. The sky flickered and they were in the garden again but otherwise alone.

17

A lice looked out of the kitchen window at Teasel, who was exploring the bounds of Astrid's back garden. Astrid seemed to have not yet come to terms with the fact that they now had a cow living with them. It was a good thing she was currently cock-a-hoop about their successful jaunt to the past.

"Oh. My. Actual. God," Astrid grinned with girlish glee. "Did we just go to a party with David Bowie?"

"We totally did," said Maddie. "The most annoying thing is that we can't tell anyone. Drinking and dancing with rock royalty. And Alice. Hey, Alice!" Maddie threw a cushion from the lounge to get her attention. "Alice, you are the inspiration behind a classic song; you have no idea how big a deal that is! Put it on, Astrid. Alexa: play *Rebel, Rebel.*"

"You know I don't allow any of that spy software in my house," said Astrid. "Let me find the vinyl, it's the only way to appreciate it." She went off to rifle through a cupboard.

"Show us the song lyrics, Alice," said Maddie. "I can't believe you sort of co-wrote it. We can sell that for tens of thousands."

Alice reached into her pocket. "Oh. Bodkins."

"Yes! Bodkins! David seemed to love that."

"No, I mean it. Bodkins. Look." She thrust her hand into the pocket of her dress and her fingertips came wiggling out of the bottom. "I put it in my pocket..."

"Alice, you ripped your dress," Maddie whispered. "Alice, your face is a mess."

"We lost the paper he wrote the song on?" said Astrid. She looked stricken.

"It's probably in a garden in seventeen twenty-something," said Alice.

"We could go look..." said Maddie.

"No – no it's fine," said Astrid with weary sadness. She immediately straightened up and forced a more positive expression onto her face. "But bloody hell, we met David Bowie. Right?"

"Exactly," said Alice. "Can I still hear the song though, please?"

As Astrid sorted through her shelf of records, Alice looked to the kitchen again, and the garden beyond. "Are we like Miss Piggy?"

"Pardon?" said Maddie.

"It feels like nearly everything we've done we were fated to do. Rescuing Teasel. Saving you at that ball by poisoning the drink. They only happened because we knew they were going to happen. Are we being controlled?"

"Are you asking me if a puppeteer has their hand up our

arses, controlling our every action? I think I would have noticed."

"Free will is an illusion," said Astrid, still looking for her record.

"Ignore her," said Maddie. "She's a bitter and disillusioned nihilist."

"I just want to know if we can ever change anything," said Alice.

"I don't know," said Maddie.

Alice picked up Master Burnleigh's woollen tunic from the side where she'd put it. "The Master Burnleigh in my time is the same man we saw in seventeen-twenty. He whisked the man, Chamberlain, away and had me sentenced to burn at the stake." She swallowed hard against the emotions within her. "If it wasn't for him, my Granny Merrial wouldn't have died. So, I ask, can we change things?"

"Sure we can," said Astrid. "We saved that idiot biker's life, didn't we?"

"Exactly," said Maddie. She looked at her phone.

"Here," said Astrid, pulling out a record with a painted image of an older and stranger David Bowie on the cover. "Let's take a listen."

"Shit," Maddie tutted.

"What?" said Astrid.

Maddie held out her phone, then before Alice could even glimpse what was on the screen, took it back to read.

"Tragic accident ... young motorcyclist ... overtook a car at Tickley traffic island and rode into the path of a delivery lorry ... confirmed dead at the scene."

"When?" said Astrid.

"The Friday afternoon."

Astrid coughed out a laugh. "Friday. So – Wednesday, Thursday, Friday. Each time, we give him a day. Pointless."

Alice instantly thought about that moment when she had gone back and squatted outside the cow byre and heard her granny's voice again. What wouldn't she give for just one more day with Merrial?

"One day is not pointless," she said firmly. "Put your record on, Astrid. Music we can dance to. Today we dance and tomorrow we save Skid again. Is there anything in the house for us to drink?"

"Girl's thinking on my wavelength," said Maddie, jumping up to go see if there were any beers in the fridge.

ABOUT THE AUTHOR

Heide Goody lives in North Warwickshire with her family and pets. Iain Grant lives in South Birmingham with his family and pets.

They are both married but not to each other.

ALSO BY HEIDE GOODY

Clovenhoof

Getting fired can ruin a day...

...especially when you were the Prince of Hell.

Will Satan survive in English suburbia?

Corporate life can be a soul draining experience, especially when the industry is Hell, and you're Lucifer. It isn't all torture and brimstone, though, for the Prince of Darkness, he's got an unhappy Board of Directors.

The numbers look bad.

They want him out.

Then came the corporate coup.

Banished to mortal earth as Jeremy Clovenhoof, Lucifer is going through a mid-immortality crisis of biblical proportion. Maybe if he just tries to blend in, it won't be so bad.

He's wrong.

If it isn't the murder, cannibalism, and armed robbery of everyday life in Birmingham, it's the fact that his heavy metal band isn't getting the respect it deserves, that's dampening his mood.

And the archangel Michael constantly snooping on him, doesn't help.

If you enjoy clever writing, then you'll adore this satirical tour de force, because a good laugh can make you have sympathy for the devil.

Get it now.

Clovenhoof

Oddjobs

Unstoppable horrors from beyond are poised to invade and literally create Hell on Earth.

It's the end of the world as we know it, but someone still needs to do the paperwork.

Morag Murray works for the secret government organisation responsible for making sure the apocalypse goes as smoothly and as quietly as possible.

Trouble is, Morag's got a temper problem and, after angering the wrong alien god, she's been sent to another city where she won't cause so much trouble.

But Morag's got her work cut out for her. She has to deal with a man-eating starfish, solve a supernatural murder and, if she's got time, prevent her own inevitable death.

If you like The Laundry Files, The Chronicles of St Mary's or Men in Black, you'll love the Oddjobs series."If Jodi Taylor wrote a Laundry Files novel set it in Birmingham... A hilarious dose of bleak existential despair. With added tentacles! And bureaucracy!" – Charles Stross, author of The Laundry Files series.

Oddjobs

Printed in Great Britain
by Amazon

30251344R00058